A Little Princess

Frances Hodgson Burnett

Condensed and Adapted by
LOUISE COLLN

Illustrated by
JON SAYER

Cover Illustrated by
PHILIP HOWE

Dalmatian Publishing Group

The Junior Classics have been
adapted and illustrated with care and thought
to introduce you to a world of famous authors, characters, ideas,
and great stories that have been loved for generations.

Editor — Kathryn Knight
Creative Director — Gina Rhodes-Haynes
And the entire classics project team
of Dalmatian Publishing Group

A LITTLE PRINCESS

Published in 2010 by Creative Edge, LLC,
an imprint of Dalmatian Publishing Group.
Copyright © 2010 Dalmatian Publishing Group,
Franklin, Tennessee 37067 • 1-800-815-8696

ISBN: 1-40379-506-1

Printed in the U.S.A.

CE12436/0110 CLI

FOREWORD

A note to the reader—

A classic story rests in your hands. The characters are famous. The tale is timeless.

This Junior Classic edition of *A Little Princess* has been carefully condensed and adapted from the original version (which you really *must* read when you're ready for every detail). We kept the well-known phrases for you. We kept Frances Hodgson Burnett's style. And we kept the important imagery and heart of the tale.

Literature is terrific fun! It encourages you to think. It helps you dream. It is full of heroes and villains, suspense and humor, adventure and wonder, and new ideas. It introduces you to writers who reach out across time to say: "Do you want to hear a story I wrote?"

Curl up and enjoy.

CONTENTS

1. Sara 1

2. A French Lesson 11

3. Ermengarde 19

4. Lottie 27

5. Becky 35

6. The Diamond Mines 47

7. The Diamond Mines Again 55

8. In the Attic 69

9. Melchisedec 77

10. The Indian Gentleman 89

11. Ram Dass 99

12. The Other Side of the Wall 107

13. One of the People 115

14. What Melchisedec Heard and Saw 125

15. The Magic 129

16. The Visitor 143

17. "It Is the Child" 153

18. "I Tried Not to Be" 161

19. Anne 171

    About the Author 180

SARA CREWE — a girl who knows the beauty of dreams and magic, and how to be a real princess

CAPTAIN CREWE — Sara's handsome father

MISS MINCHIN — a cold-hearted woman who runs a school for young ladies

MISS AMELIA — Miss Minchin's sister

EMILY — Sara's special doll

MARIETTE — Sara's French maid

MONSIEUR DUFARGE — the French teacher

ERMENGARDE ST. JOHN — Sara's best friend at Miss Minchin's school

BECKY — the scullery maid, Sara's fellow "prisoner" in the attic

LOTTIE LEGH — an unhappy little girl, "mothered" by Sara

CHARACTERS

LAVINIA HERBERT — a spiteful, older girl who is jealous of Sara

JESSIE — Lavinia's best friend

MR. BARROW — Captain Crewe's lawyer who brings bad news

MELCHISEDEC — Sara's pet rat that lives in the attic room wall

MR. CARRISFORD — the sad-hearted gentleman from India who moves next door

RAM DASS — a Lascar from India who lives next door and serves Mr. Carrisford

THE CARMICHAELS — the real name of the LARGE FAMILY, the eight happy children, mother and father whom Sara watches through the window. Mr. Carmichael is Mr. Carrisford's lawyer.

ANNE — the baker woman's helper, who once met Sara on a cold, rainy evening...

A Little Princess

CHAPTER ONE

Sara

Once on a dark winter's day, the yellow fog hung so thick and heavy in the streets of London that the gas lamps were lighted as if it was night. A serious, thoughtful little girl sat with her father in a cab-carriage behind slow-moving horses.

Sara Crewe was only seven, but she felt as if she had lived a long, long time. She was thinking of the sea voyage she had just made from the blazing sun of her home in India to cold, dark England. She moved closer to her father.

"What is it, darling?" The handsome, young Captain Crewe held her close.

"Is this the place, Papa?" Sara whispered.

"Yes, little Sara, it is."

She knew that he felt as sad as she did.

He was the only relative Sara had in the world, and they loved each other very much. He was rich and gave her toys and pets and everything she wanted. Her mother had died when she was born, so their many Indian servants cared for her. They bowed to her and called her "Missee Sahib," and let her have her own way in everything.

Her only unhappiness had been in knowing that she must spend several years in a boarding school in England while her father lived in India. The climate of India was very bad for children. As soon as possible they were sent away from it, usually to London or Paris, to stay at school. And now Sara was here in London.

"But you will be happy here, little Sara," her father said. "You will go to a nice house where there will be a lot of little girls to play with. I will send you plenty of books, and the time will pass very quickly."

He kissed her and held her more closely in his arms as their cab driver pulled his horses to a stop in front of the school.

It was a big, brick row-house, exactly like all the others in its square, except that on the front door a brass plate read:

MISS MINCHIN
Select Seminary for Young Ladies

They entered a hall that looked shiny and hard and were taken into a drawing room, where the floor was covered by a rug with a square pattern on it. The chairs were also square and seemed to have hard bones in them. A heavy marble clock stood upon the heavy marble mantel.

As she sat down in one of the stiff chairs, Sara looked about her.

"I don't like it, Papa," she said. "But, then, I suppose soldiers—even brave ones—don't like going into battle. So, since I am here, I must be resigned."

Captain Crewe laughed.

"Oh, little Sara," he said. "What shall I do when I have no one to say such serious things to me?"

And then suddenly he stopped laughing. He swept her into his arms and hugged her very hard, looking almost as if tears had come into his eyes.

Just then Miss Minchin entered the room. She was very like her house, Sara thought—tall and stiff and ugly. She had cold eyes, and she had a fishy smile for the rich Captain Crewe.

"It will be a great honor to have charge of such a beautiful and clever child," she said.

"Why does she say I am beautiful?" thought Sara. "I'm not beautiful at all. She is telling a lie."

Sara wasn't aware that she had an odd charm of her own. She was slim and rather tall for her age. Her short black hair curled at the tips. She had big gray-green eyes with long, black lashes. Her mouth seemed to have a smile playing about its corners, but it could also be very determined.

She stood near her father and listened while he and Miss Minchin talked. Sara was to have a pretty bedroom and sitting room of her own. She would also have a carriage and a maid.

"She is always sitting with her little nose in big grown-up books," her father said. "Send her out to buy a new doll if she reads too much."

"Papa," Sara said, "if I bought many new dolls, I would have more than I could be fond of. Dolls ought to be your dearest friends. Emily is going to be my dearest friend."

"Who is Emily?" Miss Minchin inquired.

"Emily is a doll Papa is going to buy for me," Sara said. "She's going to be my friend when Papa is gone."

Sara stayed with her father for several days at his hotel before he sailed back to India. He took her to fine shops and bought clothes that were much too grand for a child of seven. There were velvet and lace dresses, fur coats and muffs and hats, gloves and handkerchiefs and silk stockings.

They looked at a great many dolls before they found just the right "Emily."

"I want a doll who looks as if she listens when I talk to her," Sara explained.

They had passed two or three shops, when Sara suddenly clutched her father's arm.

"Oh, Papa!" she cried, pointing to a doll in the window. "There she is. There is Emily. She is actually waiting there for us. Let us go in to her."

She was a large doll with long, golden-brown, curling hair. Her eyes were blue, with real eyelashes, and she looked as if she could listen.

"Of course, Papa," Sara said, "this is Emily."

They took Emily to a children's dress shop and bought her clothes as grand as Sara's own.

The next day Captain Crewe took Sara to Miss Minchin's. He explained to Miss Minchin that his lawyer, Mr. Barrow, would pay for Sara's expenses, and she was to be given whatever she asked for.

Then Sara and her father went into Sara's own sitting room to tell each other good-bye. Sara sat on his knee and looked long and hard at his face.

"Are you learning me by heart, little Sara?" he said, stroking her hair.

"No," she answered. "I know you by heart. You are inside my heart." They held each other close until it was time for him to go.

When the cab drove away, Sara was sitting with Emily on the floor of her room, watching from her window. Miss Minchin sent her sister, Miss Amelia, to see what the child was doing, but Miss Amelia couldn't open the door.

"I have locked it," said a polite little voice from inside. "I want to be quite by myself, if you please."

Sara held Emily and watched her father's cab until it turned the corner of the square, while Captain Crewe looked backward, waving and kissing his hand as if he could not bear to stop.

CHAPTER TWO

A French Lesson

The next morning, Sara's new maid, Mariette, dressed her in a dark-blue schoolroom dress and tied her hair with a dark-blue ribbon. Sara went to Emily, who sat in a chair of her own, and put a book in her lap.

"What I believe about Emily," she explained to Mariette, "is that, really, she can read and talk and walk, but she will only do it when people are out of the room. That is her secret. If you go out of the room, she will begin to read, perhaps, or go and look out of the window. Then if she hears someone coming, she runs back and pretends she can only sit and stare."

Mariette smiled. She had already begun to like this odd little girl. She had such a charming way of saying "If you please, Mariette," and "Thank you, Mariette."

When Sara entered the schoolroom, everybody stared at her. Every pupil—from Lavinia Herbert, who was nearly thirteen, to Lottie Legh, who was just four and the baby of the school—had heard a great deal about her. Lavinia had passed Sara's room when the door was open, and had seen Mariette opening a box of her grand clothes.

"I saw her shaking out lace petticoats," Lavinia whispered to her friend Jessie. "She has got one of them on now."

"She has silk stockings on!" whispered Jessie.

"I don't think she's pretty at all," Lavinia said. "Her eyes are such a strange color."

"She isn't pretty as other pretty people are," said Jessie, looking across the room, "but she makes you want to look at her again."

Miss Minchin rapped in a grand manner upon her desk.

"Young ladies," she said, "Miss Crewe is our new pupil. I shall expect you all to be very friendly to her."

The pupils bowed. Sara made a little curtsy.

"Sara," said Miss Minchin, "as your papa has given you a French maid, I believe that he wishes you to study the French language."

Sara felt a little uncomfortable.

"I believe he just thought I would like her, Miss Minchin," replied Sara

"I am afraid," said Miss Minchin, with a slightly sour smile, "that you have been a very spoiled little girl. Do you always imagine that things are done because you like them?"

Sara felt a flush rising on her cheeks. Miss Minchin seemed to be a very stern person. Sara wasn't sure how to tell her that she and her father often spoke French to each other. Sara's mother had been a French woman, and Captain Crewe loved her language.

"I—I have never really learned French, but—but—" she began.

"That is enough," Miss Minchin said tartly. "If you have not learned, you must begin at once. The French master, Monsieur Dufarge, will be here in a few minutes. Take this book and study it until he arrives. You look rather cross. I am sorry you do not like the idea of learning French."

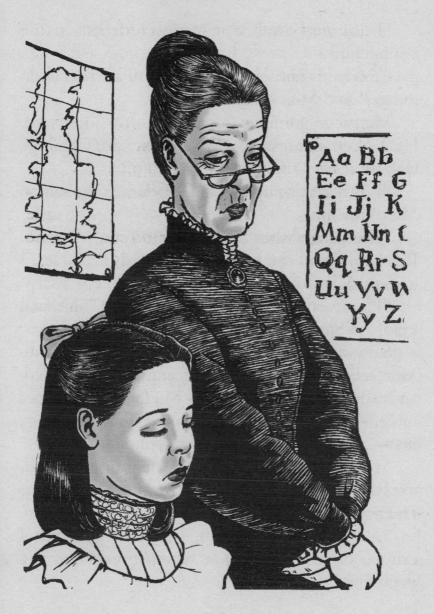

"I am very fond of it," answered Sara, trying again, "but—"

"You must not say 'but' when you are told to do things," said Miss Minchin.

Monsieur Dufarge arrived shortly afterward. He looked interested when he saw Sara politely looking at her little book of French phrases.

"Is this a new pupil for me, Madame?" he said to Miss Minchin.

"Her papa wishes that she should study French. But I am afraid she has a childish wish not to learn it," said Miss Minchin.

"I am sorry for that, Mademoiselle," he said kindly to Sara.

Sara stood beside her seat. She looked up into Monsieur Dufarge's face and explained in pretty and fluent French that Madame had not understood. She had not learned French out of books, but her papa had always spoken it to her.

Miss Minchin sat staring at her over her eyeglasses. When Sara had finished, Monsieur Dufarge took the phrase book from her.

"Ah, Madame," he said, "there is not much I can teach her. She has not *learned* French—it is a *part* of her."

"You ought to have told me," Miss Minchin said, frowning at Sara.

"I—I tried," said Sara. "I—I suppose I did not begin right."

Miss Minchin knew that it had not been Sara's fault that she was not allowed to explain. And when she saw that Lavinia and Jessie were giggling behind their French grammar books, she was even angrier.

"Silence, young ladies!" she said severely, rapping upon the desk. "Silence at once!"

And she began from that minute to feel a grudge against her new pupil.

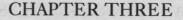

CHAPTER THREE

Ermengarde

That morning Sara noticed one little girl, about her own age, who watched her with a pair of light, rather dull, blue eyes. She was a plump child who did not seem to be clever, but she had a good-natured face. Her yellow hair was braided in a tight pigtail, tied with a ribbon. She had pulled this pigtail around her neck, and was biting the end of the ribbon.

Miss Minchin scolded her for biting her hair. Sara saw that the little girl had tears coming to her eyes.

During the French lesson, the girl's answers were so bad they made Lavinia and Jessie laugh.

Sara had a hot little temper, and it made her feel rather savage when she saw the poor, unhappy child's face. She didn't like to see anyone being made fun of. She felt sorry for the girl and wanted to be her friend.

When lessons were over and the pupils gathered to talk, Sara looked for the little girl with blue eyes. Finding her bundled in a window seat, she walked over to her and asked her name.

"My name's Ermengarde St. John," she said softly and shyly.

"Mine is Sara Crewe," said Sara. "Your name is very pretty."

"I—I like yours, too," Ermengarde said.

Miss St. John was amazed that the new girl, who had a maid and her own sitting room, would speak to her. Ermengarde knew that the other girls made fun of her. She was often in disgrace or in tears.

Sara got onto the window seat, which was a big, deep one, and sat with her hands clasped round her knees. She looked out of the window into the dingy square, where the sparrows were hopping and twittering on the wet iron railings and the sooty branches of the trees.

"You can speak French very well," Ermengarde told Sara.

"You could speak French, too, if you had always heard it."

Ermengarde shook her head so that the pigtail wobbled. "I couldn't. I can't say the words. They're so strange."

Seeing a mournful look on the chubby face, Sara changed the subject.

"Would you like to see Emily?"

"Who is Emily?" Ermengarde asked.

"Come up to my room and see," said Sara, holding out her hand.

They jumped down from the window seat and went upstairs.

"Let's be very quiet," Sara said, when they were outside her room. "Perhaps we can catch Emily watching people in the square."

She suddenly threw the door wide open. The room was quiet, with a cozy fire burning in the grate. A wonderful doll was sitting in a chair with a book in her lap.

"Oh, she got back to her seat before we could see her!" Sara explained. "Of course they always do. They are as quick as lightning."

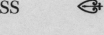

Ermengarde looked from Sara to the doll and back again.

"Can she walk?" she asked breathlessly.

"Yes," answered Sara. "At least I pretend I believe she can. And that makes it seem as if it were true. Have you never pretended things?"

"No," said Ermengarde. "Tell me about it."

"It's so beautiful that when you begin you just go on and on doing it. Emily, this is Ermengarde St. John. Ermengarde, this is Emily. Would you like to hold her?"

"Oh, yes," said Ermengarde.

Never in her dull life had Ermengarde dreamed of such an hour as the one she spent with the strange new pupil before they heard the lunch bell ring. Sara sat upon the hearth rug and told her stories of India and the voyage to England. Once a cloud passed over Sara's face and she drew her breath in with a sad little sound.

"Have you a pain?" Ermengarde asked.

"Yes," Sara answered, "but it is in my heart. I love my papa more than anything else in all the whole world ten times over. He has gone away, and I miss him so very much."

Sara put her head down on her huddled-up knees, and sat very still for a few minutes. Then she lifted her face and, with a little smile, shook back her black hair.

"If I go on telling you things about pretending, I shall bear it better," she said. "You don't forget, but you bear it better."

Ermengarde's eyes felt as if tears were in them. "Lavinia and Jessie are best friends," she said. "I wish we could be best friends. Would you have me for yours? You're clever, and I'm the stupidest child in the school, but I—oh, I do so like you!"

"I'm glad of that," said Sara. "It feels good to be liked. Yes. We will be friends. And I'll tell you what. I can help you with your French lessons."

CHAPTER FOUR

Lottie

Privately Miss Minchin disliked Sara, but she didn't want to do or say anything that might make such a rich pupil wish to leave her school. So Sara was treated more like a guest than a pupil. She was praised for everything she did. She might have become lazy and bossy, but she didn't.

"If you have everything you want and everyone is kind to you, how can you not be good-tempered?" she said to Ermengarde. "I don't know how I shall ever find out whether I am really a good child. Perhaps I'm a horrid child, and no one will ever know, just because I never have any troubles."

"Lavinia has no troubles," said Ermengarde, "and she is horrid enough."

Lavinia was very jealous of Sara and very spiteful. Lavinia had always felt she was the leader among the girls. And she had always been the best-dressed pupil when the Select Seminary walked out to church. Now Miss Minchin put Sara, in her beautiful clothes, at the head of the line. This had been bitter enough, but Lavinia soon saw that Sara was a leader among the girls, too.

Sara was a friendly little soul. She never acted "grand," and she always shared her things. She was very kind to the youngest pupils, and when one of the littlest cried, she hugged her and gave her a treat. She and Emily sometimes had tea parties for them with Emily's tiny cups and plates with the blue flowers on them.

Lottie Legh adored Sara. Lottie, who was almost five, had been sent to school because her papa did not know what to do with her after her mother died. She was badly spoiled and she wept and howled whenever she didn't get her own way.

One morning Sara heard Miss Amelia and Miss Minchin trying to silence Lottie's angry wails.

"I haven't got any mam—ma-a!" Lottie howled.

"What *is* she crying for," yelled Miss Minchin.

"Oh, Lottie!" Miss Amelia screeched. "Do stop, darling! Don't cry! Please don't!"

"Oh! Oh! Oh!" Lottie cried over and over. "I haven't—got—any—mam—ma-a!"

When Sara entered the room, Lottie was lying on the floor, screaming and kicking her small fat legs, and Miss Amelia was bending over her.

"I came over," explained Sara, "because I thought, perhaps, I could get Lottie to be quiet. May I try? I'll stay with her."

Miss Amelia was glad to leave the child to Sara.

Sara sat down flat on the floor beside the howling child without saying anything. Except for Lottie's angry screams, the room was quiet. This was new to Lottie. She opened her tight-shut eyes. She thought she might begin her tantrum again, but the quiet of the room and Sara's calm face made her howl rather half-heartedly.

"I—haven't—any—ma—ma—ma-a!"

"Neither have I," Sara answered gently.

Lottie dropped her legs and stared. She was a pretty, little, curly-headed girl and her round eyes were like wet, blue forget-me-nots. After a sulky sob, she said, "Where is she?"

"She went to heaven," Sara said. "But I am sure she comes out sometimes to see me—though I don't see her. So does yours. Perhaps they can both see us now."

Lottie sat up and looked about her. If her mamma had seen her tantrum, her mamma might not think Lottie was acting like the child of a heavenly angel.

Sara went on talking about heaven. She seemed to be telling a real story about a lovely country where real people were.

"There are fields and fields of lilies," she said, as if in a dream, "and the soft wind blows over them and sends the scent into the air. And little children run about in the lily fields and gather armfuls of them. And people are never tired, however far they walk. And there are pearl walls all round the city, but they are low enough for the people to go and lean over them. The people look down onto the earth and smile, and send beautiful messages."

Lottie listened, and then cried again. "I—haven't any mamma in this school."

Sara took hold of the chubby hand and pulled her close to her side.

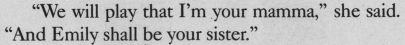
"We will play that I'm your mamma," she said. "And Emily shall be your sister."

Lottie suddenly showed her dimples.

"Will she?" she said.

"Yes," answered Sara, jumping to her feet. "Let's go and tell her. And then I'll wash your face and brush your hair."

Lottie agreed quite cheerfully. She trotted out of the room and upstairs with her.

And from that time on, Sara was an adopted mother.

CHAPTER FIVE

Becky

Sara had been at Miss Minchin's school about two years when she caught sight of a dingy little figure standing on the school steps, watching her get out of her carriage. Sara smiled at the smudgy face peeping at her through the railings of the steps. But the wide-eyed child dodged out of sight, scurrying through the kitchen door.

That evening, Sara was telling a story to a group of girls who had gathered around her in the schoolroom. Sara loved to tell stories. She forgot that she was talking to other children. She seemed to live with the fairy folk or the princes and princesses she told about.

She was creating a story that night about a princess who went to live with a prince merman in shining caves under the sea. The child who had peeped through the railings entered the room. She was carrying a coal bucket that was much too heavy for her. She knelt on the hearth rug and put pieces of coal on the fire carefully, and then she brushed around the fire irons very quietly. Sara saw that she was doing her work slowly to hear the story, so Sara raised her voice.

"The mermaids swam softly about in the crystal-green water, and dragged after them a fishing net woven of deep-sea pearls," she said.

The small servant girl swept the hearth again and again. At last the story so charmed her that she forgot that she was a servant who needed to be doing her work. The brush hung loosely in her fingers. The storyteller's voice went on and drew her into winding caves under the sea, glowing with soft, clear blue light, and paved with pure golden sands. Strange sea flowers and grasses waved about her, and far away faint singing and music echoed.

The hearth brush fell from the work-roughened hand.

Lavinia looked around. "That servant girl has been listening," she said.

The servant girl scrambled to her feet. She grabbed the coal bucket and ran out of the room.

"Why shouldn't she listen?" Sara said, frowning at Lavinia.

"Well," said Lavinia as she tossed her head, "I do not know whether your mamma would like you to tell stories to servant girls, but I know *my* mamma wouldn't like *me* to do it."

"My mamma, I'm sure, wouldn't mind in the least," Sara quietly said. "She knew that stories belong to everyone."

That night, Sara sat thinking at the little table in her room. She asked Mariette about the girl who tended the fires.

"Her name is Becky," Mariette told her. "She is a sad little thing who has just become the scullery maid. She scrubs floors and cleans windows and carries coal. She is ordered about by Cook and everybody. 'Becky do this! Becky do that!' She is fourteen years old, but only looks about twelve from being hungry all her life. She is easily frightened and looks as if she *still* never has quite enough to eat, the poor little girl."

One of Becky's chores was to put all the bedrooms in order. There were a great many of them, and she was always tired from her other work by the time she climbed the stairs to straighten the bedrooms.

She always saved Sara's rooms until last. She would sit in Sara's soft chair for a while and look about her at the beautiful things. On one chilly afternoon, she was so tired that she fell asleep as she sat there.

When Sara came in from a dancing lesson, there was Becky—with a coal smudge on her nose and several on her apron, with her cap hanging half off her head, and an empty coal bucket on the rug beside her—fast asleep in the soft chair.

"Oh!" cried Sara. "The poor thing!"

Just then a piece of coal broke off from a large lump and fell on the grate. Becky opened her eyes with a gasp. She sprang up and clutched at her cap, trying wildly to put it straight.

"Oh, miss! Oh, miss! I ask yer pardon, miss! Oh, I do, miss!"

"Don't be frightened," Sara said.

"I didn't mean to do it, miss. It was the warm fire—and me bein' so tired."

Sara put her hand on Becky's shoulder.

"You were tired. You couldn't help it."

Becky stared at her. "Ain't yer angry, miss?" she gasped. "Ain't yer goin' to tell the missus?"

"No," cried Sara. "Of course I'm not."

She put her hand against Becky's cheek.

"Why," she said, "you are only a little girl just like me. It's just an accident that I am me, and you are you!"

"A' accident, miss," Becky repeated. "Is it?" She didn't quite understand this kind girl's words.

Sara opened her door, looked out, and listened.

"No one is about. Perhaps you might stay a while. Perhaps you might like a piece of cake."

The next ten minutes seemed to Becky too full of joy to believe. Sara gave her a thick slice of cake. They talked and laughed until Becky began to feel less fearful.

"Is that—" she asked, looking longingly at the rose-colored dancing dress Sara was wearing. "Is that there your best?"

"It is one of my dancing frocks," answered Sara. "Do you like it?"

For a few seconds, Becky was silent. Then she said in an awed voice, "Once I saw a princess.

I was in the street, watching the rich people goin' by. The crowd all says at once, 'That's the princess.' She was a growed-up young lady who threw gold coins to us. She was pink all over— gown an' cloak, an' flowers an' all. I thought of her the minnit I see you, miss. You look like her."

"I would like to be a princess," said Sara. "I believe I will begin pretending I am one. Were you listening to my story in the schoolroom?"

"Yes, miss. I knowed I wasn't s'posed to, but it was so beautiful, I—I couldn't help it."

"Would you like to hear the rest?"

"Me hear it?" Becky cried. "Like as if I was a pupil, miss? All about the prince—and the little white mer-babies swimming about laughing—with stars in their hair?"

Sara nodded. "I'll try to be here when you do my rooms. I'll tell you a little bit of it every day."

"Then," breathed Becky, "I wouldn't mind how heavy the coal buckets was—or what the cook done to me, if—if I might have that to think of."

When Becky went downstairs, she had an extra piece of cake in her pocket. She had been fed and warmed as much by Sara's friendliness as by the cake and fire.

When Becky was gone, Sara sat with her chin in her hands.

"If I were a princess—a real princess," she thought, "I would do good deeds to help the people. Doing nice things for people is the same as throwing gold coins and gifts into the street. But even if I am only a *pretend* princess, I can think of little things to do for people. Things like sharing stories and cake with Becky. She was just as happy as if it was coins. I'll pretend that doing things people like is the same as scattering gold. So, today I've scattered gold."

CHAPTER SIX

The Diamond Mines

Not long after this, Sara received a special letter from her father. A friend who had been at school with him was the owner of land upon which diamonds had been found. Because they were friends, he was letting Captain Crewe become a partner. Captain Crewe was giving all his money to his friend for his part of the mines.

All the girls listened that afternoon as Sara created stories of passages deep in the earth, where stones shone from the walls. They were just like tales from the *Arabian Nights*!

Lavinia told Jessie that she didn't believe diamond mines existed.

"If there were mines full of diamonds, people would be as rich as princes and princesses," sniffed Lavinia.

"Perhaps Sara will be as rich as a princess," giggled Jessie. "She likes to pretend that she is a princess."

"I suppose she thinks she could be a princess even if she was a beggar," said Lavinia.

Sara looked up. She controlled her anger, for she knew that a princess does not fly into a rage.

"It's true," Sara said. "Sometimes I do pretend I am a princess. I pretend I am a princess so that I can try to behave like one."

Lavinia didn't know quite what to think about this. "Dear me!" she said. "I hope, Princess Sara, that when you sit upon your throne you won't forget us!"

"I won't," said Sara.

At that, Lavinia and Jessie left the room

To Becky, Sara *was* a real princess. Miss Minchin knew that Sara was kind to Becky, but she didn't know about the times that she spent in Sara's sitting room. Sara told Becky stories and gave her food to eat there and food to take up to her room in the attic.

"But I has to eat 'em careful, miss," Becky said. "If I leaves crumbs the rats come out to get 'em."

"Rats!" exclaimed Sara. "Are there rats there?"

"Lots of 'em, miss," Becky answered. "There mostly is rats an' mice in attics. You gets used to the noise they make running about. I've got so I don't mind 'em as long as they don't run over my pillow. You gets used to anythin' after a while. You have to, miss, if you're born a scullery maid."

Now when Sara went out, she brought home small things like little meat pies to give her hungry friend. Becky's eyes sparkled when she saw them.

"Oh, miss!" she murmured. "Them will be nice an' filling. It's fillingness that's best. Sponge cake's a heavenly thing, but it doesn't stay. These'll just stay in yer stummick."

In time, Becky began to lose her hungry, tired feeling. The coal box didn't seem so heavy and it didn't matter how much work she was given to do, or how much the cook scolded her. She always had the afternoon to look forward to. And she could always remember her special times with Sara as she lay awake in her attic bed.

Nature had made Sara a giver. If nature has made you a giver, your hands are born open, and so is your heart. There may be times when your hands are empty, but your heart is always full. You can give things out of that. Warm things, kind things, sweet things—help and comfort and laughter.

Becky had scarcely known what laughter was through all her poor, hard-driven life. Sara made her laugh, and laughed with her. And, though neither of them quite knew it, the laughter was as "filling" as the meat pies.

·⊹§⬦3⊹·

A few weeks before Sara's eleventh birthday, a letter came from her father that did not seem to be written in such high spirits as usual. He was not feeling very well, and was troubled by the business of the diamond mines.

But he had wonderful plans and surprises for Sara's birthday. Among other things, a new doll had been ordered in Paris, and her wardrobe was to be splendid. Sara wrote back that she was too old for dolls—so she would call it the Last Doll.

The morning of her birthday, Sara found a small, dumpy package, tied up in a piece of brown paper, on her table. She opened it happily. It was a square pincushion, made of not-quite-clean red flannel, with black pins stuck carefully into it to form the words, "Menny hapy returns."

"Oh!" cried Sara. "How hard Becky has worked on this."

She heard the door being slowly pushed open. Becky peeped in with a loving grin on her face.

"Do yer like it, Miss Sara?" she said. "Do yer?"

"Like it?" cried Sara. "You darling Becky, you made it all yourself."

Becky's eyes teared up with delight. "It ain't nothin' but flannel, an' the flannel ain't new. But I wanted to give yer somethin' an' I made it up nights. I knew yer could pretend it was satin with diamond pins in. I tried to pretend when I was makin' it."

Sara hugged her. She felt tears in her eyes, too, from knowing how hard Becky had worked. It was a better present even than all the big ones she was to get later. "I love you, Becky—I do, I do!"

"Oh, miss!" breathed Becky. "Thank yer, miss, kindly. It ain't good enough for that. The—the flannel wasn't new."

CHAPTER SEVEN

The Diamond Mines Again

Miss Minchin had the schoolroom decorated grandly for Sara's birthday. Sara opened her presents, and then all the girls were invited to Miss Minchin's very own sitting room for a special feast. The pupils were excited about the presents, especially a baby-size doll.

"Here is her clothes trunk," said Sara. "Let's open it and look at the Last Doll's things."

She sat down upon the floor and lifted out tray after tray of jewels and clothes.

"Suppose," she said, "just suppose she understands us and feels proud of being beautiful."

"You're always pretending things," said Lavinia.

"I know I am," answered Sara. "I like to pretend. If you pretend hard enough, it seems to be real."

"It's all very well to pretend things if you have everything," said Lavinia. "Could you pretend if you were a beggar and lived in an attic?"

Sara looked thoughtful. "I believe I could," she said. "But it might not be easy."

Meanwhile, as the girls were enjoying the party in Miss Minchin's sitting room, Miss Minchin was having a meeting in the schoolroom with Captain Crewe's lawyer, Mr. Barrow.

He had come to tell her that Sara's father had lost all his money in the diamond mines. But the saddest news was that Sara's dear papa was dead.

"He put all his money into his friend's mines. Then the friend ran away. Captain Crewe was already ill with jungle fever when the news came. The shock was too much for him. He died raving about his little girl—and hadn't a penny to leave her."

Miss Minchin gave no thought to how sad Sara would be. She only thought about the money.

"Do you mean to tell me," she cried out, "that the spoiled, fanciful child is left on my hands a little beggar instead of a rich heiress? Her father owes me money for all her birthday gifts!"

"Yes. She is surely left on your hands, ma'am—as she hasn't a relative that we know of."

Miss Minchin gasped. "I won't house and feed the little beggar. I have been robbed and cheated. I will turn her out into the street!"

Mr. Barrow moved toward the door and said, "I wouldn't do that, madam. It wouldn't look well. It would be a bad story to get out about the school. Better keep her and make use of her."

Miss Minchin was so angry that she called Miss Amelia in and sent her to stop the party. Miss Amelia was sorry for Sara, but she always did what her sister told her to do. Sara was told the sad news cruelly in front of all the girls. Miss Amelia ended by telling Sara to go up to her room and put on the only black dress she owned, even though it was now too small for her.

Sara stood still without making a sound. Her eyes got bigger and bigger, and she went pale. She stood staring for a few seconds, and then she ran upstairs. Some of the other children started crying, and Miss Amelia sent them to their rooms.

Sara hardly remembered anything but walking up and down, saying over and over again to herself, "My papa is dead! My papa is dead!"

But she wasn't given any time to cry before Miss Minchin sent for her. When she came into Miss Minchin's sitting room, Sara's face was white. She held her mouth shut tightly to keep it from trembling. She did not look or feel like the child who had been given everything she wanted. It seemed as if her birthday party had happened long ago in the life of quite another little girl.

She had on the black dress. She held Emily tightly in one arm, wrapped in some black cloth.

Miss Minchin looked stern and unkind. "Put down your doll," she said.

"No," Sara answered. "I will not put her down. She is all I have. My papa gave her to me."

Miss Minchin found it hard to look at Sara, perhaps because she knew how cruelly she was treating Sara.

"You will have no time for dolls," she said. "Everything will be very different now."

"Yes," answered Sara. "My papa is dead. He left me no money. I am quite poor."

"You are a beggar," said Miss Minchin. "You are quite alone in the world and have no one to do anything for you, unless I choose to keep you here out of charity."

For a moment the pale little face trembled. "I understand," answered Sara, very bravely. "I understand."

Miss Minchin was a bully and she wanted to make Sara cry.

"Don't put on grand airs," she said. "You are not a princess any longer. Your carriage and your maid will be sent away. You will wear your oldest and plainest clothes. You are like Becky—you must work for your living."

To her surprise, a look of relief came into the child's eyes.

"Can I work?" Sara said. "What can I do?"

"You can do anything you are told," was the answer. "If you are useful I may let you stay here. You will help the younger children with French lessons and run errands and help in the kitchen, too. If you don't please me, you will be sent away. Remember that. Now go."

Sara stood still for a moment, looking at her. Then she turned to leave the room.

"Stop!" said Miss Minchin. "Don't you intend to thank me?"

Sara paused. "What for?" she said.

"For my kindness in giving you a home."

Sara made two or three steps toward her. Her thin little chest heaved up and down, and she spoke in an un-childishly fierce way.

"You are not kind," she said. "And it is not a home." She turned and ran out of the room.

Sara went up the stairs slowly, holding Emily tightly. Just before she reached her room, Miss Amelia came out of it.

"You—you are not to go in there," Miss Amelia said, looking ashamed and sad. "This is not your room now."

"Where is my room?" Sara asked, hoping that her voice didn't shake.

"You are to sleep in the attic next to Becky."

Without answering, Sara turned away. She climbed two flights of stairs. The last one was narrow and covered with torn carpet. She was leaving the world where the other child, who she used to be, had lived. Now she was someone else.

When she reached the attic door and opened it, her heart gave a dreary little thump. She shut the door and looked about her.

The room had a slanting roof. The paint on the walls was dirty and had fallen off in places. There was a rusty grate with no fire, and a hard bed with a faded blanket. A table and a red footstool with a crooked leg stood under a window in the roof. Sara sat down on the footstool. She put her arms around Emily, and dropped her face down upon her, not making a sound.

Her door was timidly pushed open and Becky's tear-smeared face peeped round it.

"Oh, miss," she said. "Might I jest come in?"

Sara lifted her head and looked at her. She tried to smile, but somehow she could not. She held out her hand and gave a little sob.

"Oh, Becky," she said. "I told you we were just the same—just two little girls. There's no difference now. I'm not a princess anymore."

Becky ran to her and caught her hand. "Yes, miss, you are," she cried, "Whats'ever 'appens to you—whats'ever—you'd be a princess all the same—an' nothin' couldn't make you nothin' different."

CHAPTER EIGHT

In the Attic

Sara never forgot the first night she spent in her attic.

"My papa is dead!" she kept whispering to herself. "My papa is dead!"

She turned over and over in her hard bed to find a place to rest. The wind howled over the roof and it was the darkest place she had ever been in. She heard the scratching and squeaking of rats and mice in the walls.

When the night finally ended and she went down to breakfast, she saw that Lavinia sat at Miss Minchin's side, in what used to be Sara's special chair.

"You will sit with the younger children and keep them quiet, Sara," Miss Minchin said coldly.

Day by day Sara's duties increased, but she never complained. She tramped through the wet streets, carrying boxes and baskets. The cook and the housemaids enjoyed ordering her about. The pupils spoke to her as if she were a servant.

As the year went on, Sara grew taller, her worn-out frocks grew shorter, and her shoes had holes. She was told to eat in the kitchen because she was so shabby. She taught lessons, but was given none of her own. She could only study alone in the schoolroom at night after her day's work was done.

There were hours when her child heart might have broken if not for three friends.

The first was Becky. At night in her attic room Sara could hear rats scuffle and squeak within the wall. But she felt comfort in knowing that Becky was on the other side of that wall. They had little chance to speak to each other during the day.

"Don't mind me, miss," Becky told her, "if I don't say nothin' polite. Someone'd be angry at us if I did. I means 'please' an' 'thank you' an' 'beg pardon,' but I dare not take time to say it."

Before daybreak, Becky would slip into Sara's attic room to see if Sara needed any help before she went to light the fires. And when night came, Sara always heard Becky's knock at her door.

The second dear friend was Ermengarde. She had huddled in the window seat in the schoolroom and stared out of the window unhappily after Sara had moved upstairs. It was several weeks before she found the courage to come to her best and dearest friend.

Then one night when Sara went to her attic, Ermengarde was sitting on the battered footstool, dressed in her nightgown and wrapped up in a red shawl.

"Ermie!" cried Sara. "You'll get in trouble."

Ermengarde's eyes and nose were pink from crying. "I know I shall if I'm found out," she said. "But I don't care a bit. Oh, Sara, I miss you."

Something in her kind voice made a lump rise in Sara's throat. "I miss you, too," she answered.

Ermengarde opened her wet eyes wide. "I thought you had changed. You just passed me by if we met in the hall."

Sara thought a moment. "I have changed but not in my feelings for you. Miss Minchin doesn't want me to talk to the girls. Most of them don't want to talk to me. I thought—perhaps—you didn't. So I tried to keep out of your way."

"I couldn't bear it any more," Ermengarde said. "So tonight I thought of creeping up here and begging you to let us be friends again."

Sara hugged her. "You're nicer than I am," she said. "I was too proud to be friends. You see, now that troubles have come, they have shown that I am not a nice child. I was afraid they would. Perhaps that is what they were sent for."

"I don't see any good in having troubles," said Ermengarde.

"Neither do I," Sara admitted frankly. "But I suppose there might be good in most things, even if we don't see it."

Ermengarde looked at the room, her eyes wide. "Sara," she said, "can you bear living here?"

"If I pretend it's quite different, I can," Sara said, "or if I pretend it is a place in a story." She spoke slowly. Her imagination was coming back. "People have lived in worse places. Think of the Count of Monte Cristo in the dungeon! And think of the people in the Bastille, the French prison!"

"The Bastille," whispered Ermengarde. She remembered stories that Sara had told her of the people who were kept in that terrible jail during the French Revolution.

"The Bastille will be a good place to pretend about," said Sara. "I am a prisoner in the Bastille. I have been here for years and years and everybody has forgotten about me. Miss Minchin is the jailer. And Becky is the prisoner in the next cell. I shall pretend that, and it will be a great comfort."

"And will you tell me all about it?" Ermengarde asked eagerly. "May I visit you again at night?"

"Yes," answered Sara. "Bad things that happen test people, and this has tested you and proved how nice you are."

CHAPTER NINE

Melchisedec

The third person to comfort Sara was Lottie. The little girl still couldn't understand why Sara wore old clothes and came into the schoolroom only to teach.

But Lottie was a determined little person. Late one afternoon she started climbing the stairs, until she reached the attic floor. She opened a door and saw Sara standing upon an old table and looking out a window.

"Sara!" she cried. "Why are you in such an ugly room?"

Sara jumped down from her table and ran to the child.

"It's not such a bad room, Lottie," Sara said, hugging her. "You can see all sorts of things you can't see downstairs."

"What sort of things?" demanded Lottie.

"Chimneys—quite close to us—with smoke curling up in wreaths into the sky—and sparrows hopping about and talking to each other."

"Oh, let me see it!" cried Lottie.

Sara lifted her up. They stood on the old table together and leaned on the edge of the flat window in the roof.

The slate roof slanted down to the rain gutter. Sparrows perched on the chimney top. Another attic window next to hers was shut because the row-house next door was empty.

"I wish someone lived there," said Sara. "It is so close that if there was a little girl in the attic, we could talk through the window and climb over to see each other, if we were not afraid of falling."

"Oh, Sara!" cried Lottie. "I like this attic! It's nicer than downstairs!"

"Look at that sparrow," whispered Sara. "I wish I had some crumbs to throw to him."

"I have part of a bun in my pocket," said Lottie.

They threw out a few crumbs and the sparrow hopped toward them. Then he stopped as if thinking that Sara and Lottie might turn out to be big cats waiting to jump on him. At last he hopped to the biggest crumb and ate it. Soon other sparrows came. They twittered and chattered before they ate all the crumbs and flew away.

When the girls got down off the table, Sara pointed out many good things about the room.

"It is so little and so high above everything," she said, "that it is almost like a nest in a tree. When the morning begins I can lie in bed and look right up into the sky through the window in the roof. If the sun is going to shine, little pink clouds float about. And if it rains, the drops patter and patter as if they were saying something nice. If there are stars at night, you can try to count them. If that rusty grate in the corner was polished and there was a fire in it, just think how nice it would be."

But when Lottie went downstairs again, Sara sat down on the crooked stool and let her head drop in her hands.

"It's a lonely place," she said. "It's the loneliest place in the world."

She was sitting in this way when she heard a little sound near her. She lifted her head. A large rat was sitting up, sniffing the air. Some of Lottie's crumbs had dropped upon the floor and they had drawn the rat out of his hole.

He looked like a gray-whiskered dwarf or gnome, and seemed to be as frightened of Sara as she was of him.

Sara watched him for a while. "I think it is rather hard to be a rat. People jump and scream out, 'Oh, a horrid rat!' I wouldn't like people to scream and jump and say, 'Oh, a horrid Sara!' when they see me. It's different to be a sparrow. But nobody asked this rat if he wanted to be a rat when he was made. Nobody said, 'Wouldn't you rather be a sparrow?' Nobody asked me if I wanted to live in an attic."

Then she said to the rat, "Come and get the crumbs. Prisoners in the Bastille used to make friends with rats. Can I make friends with you?"

Perhaps there is a language that is not made of words, and everything in the world understands it. For somehow the rat seemed to understand Sara and knew from that moment that he was safe. He began to eat the crumbs.

A week or so later, Ermengarde tapped on the door, and she heard a low laugh and Sara's happy voice.

"There! Take it and go home, Melchisedec!"

"Who are you talking to, Sara?" Ermengarde gasped out when Sara opened the door.

Sara drew her into the attic room. "It was Melchisedec, my rat," she said, laughing.

Ermengarde landed in the middle of the bed in one bound. She tucked her feet under her nightgown.

"Oh!" she cried. "A rat!"

"Don't be frightened," said Sara. "We're good friends. I bring him scraps of food from the kitchen. Now watch!"

She made several low, whistling sounds and dropped some crumbs onto the floor. Melchisedec came out and ate them. He took a larger piece back inside the wall.

"You see," said Sara, "that is for his wife and children. At least I like to think that."

Ermengarde began to laugh.

"Oh, Sara!" she said. "You talk about Melchisedec as if he was a person."

Sara nodded. "He gets hungry and frightened, just as we do. Besides," she said, "he is a Bastille rat sent to be my friend."

"Do you always pretend it is the Bastille?"

"Nearly always," answered Sara. "Sometimes I try to pretend it's another kind of place, but the Bastille is easiest."

There were two knocks on the wall.

"What is that?" Ermengarde exclaimed.

"It's the prisoner in the next jail cell."

"Becky?" cried Ermengarde.

"Yes," said Sara. "The two knocks meant, 'Prisoner, are you there?' "

Sara knocked three times on the wall. "That means, 'Yes, I am here, and all is well.' "

Four knocks came back from Becky's side of the wall.

"That means, 'Then, fellow prisoner, we will sleep in peace. Good night.' "

"Oh, Sara!" Ermengarde whispered joyfully. "It is like a story!"

"It *is* a story," said Sara. "*Everything* is a story. You are a story—I am a story. Miss Minchin is a story."

And Sara sat down again and talked and told stories until Ermengarde forgot that *she* was a sort of escaped prisoner herself. She had to be reminded by Sara that she could not remain in the Bastille all night, but must quietly go downstairs again and creep back into her empty, waiting bed.

CHAPTER TEN

The Indian Gentleman

Ermengarde and Lottie could not visit often, so Sara lived a strange and lonely life. It was a lonelier life when she was downstairs than when she was in her attic. She had no one to talk to.

When she walked through the streets on her errands, she often had to hold onto her hat while the wind blew. The water soaked her shoes and her basket was so heavy. The crowds hurrying past her made her feel even lonelier. Sometimes she passed a shop window with a mirror in it, and she almost laughed when she saw herself. Her shabby clothes were too small for her. She would bite her lip and turn away.

In the evening on the way home, she passed row-houses on her square whose windows were lit. She used to look into the warm rooms and imagine things about the families she saw sitting before the fires or around the tables.

The family she liked best she called the Large Family, as there were so many of them. There were eight playful, happy children in the Large Family, a stout, rosy mother, and a stout, rosy father. "I'm fond of them," Sara told Becky, "and I've given them fancy names from books." She especially liked Guy Clarence, about age five, and his older sisters, Veronica Eustacia and Rosalind Gladys.

One evening the children were going to their carriage just as Sara was about to pass their door. Guy Clarence was following Veronica Eustacia and Rosalind Gladys. He was such a darling little boy, with a little round head covered with curls, that Sara paused to look at him.

It was Christmas time, and the Large Family had been hearing stories about children who were cold and hungry until kind people helped them. The little boy wanted so much to find a poor child and give her a whole sixpence, which he was *sure* would take care of her for life. He saw Sara in her shabby clothes and walked up to her.

"Here, poor little girl," he said. "Here is a sixpence. I will give it to you."

Sara's face went red. "Oh, no, thank you but I mustn't take it!" she said.

But Guy Clarence was determined to help the poor. He pushed the sixpence into her hand.

"Yes, you must take it, poor little girl!" he insisted. "You can buy things to eat with it. It is a whole sixpence!"

Sara understood that he would be heartbroken if she didn't take it. She put her pride away and said, "Thank you. You are a kind little darling."

As the boy scrambled into the carriage, Sara went away with tears in her eyes. Until now she had not known that she might be taken for a beggar.

Sara didn't know it, but the boy and his sisters were talking about her.

"I'm sure that girl was not a beggar. I was afraid she might be angry with you," said a sister.

"She wasn't angry. She said I was a kind little darling. And I was! It was my whole sixpence."

"A beggar girl would never have said that," said the other sister. "She would have said, 'Thank yer kindly, little gentleman.'"

From that time on, the children were as interested in Sara as she was in them. They called her "The-Little-Girl-who-is-not-a-beggar."

When Sara got to her room that night, she used a nail to put a hole through the coin. Then she hung it on a ribbon around her neck. It made her feel even fonder of the Large Family.

One night Sara came up to the attic cold and hungry with a raging storm in her heart. She had been sent on long errands through wind and cold and rain, and sent out again after she came in wet and hungry. Nobody cared that her young legs might be tired and her small body might be chilled. She was given only harsh words and cold looks for thanks.

"I can't bear this," said the poor child to Emily. "I'm cold. I'm wet. I'm starving to death. I've walked a thousand miles today. I couldn't find what Cook wanted, so Miss Minchin wouldn't give me any supper. Some men laughed at me because my old shoes made me slip down in the mud. My dress is covered with mud now.

Do you hear? Of course you don't hear. You are nothing but a *doll*. Nothing but a doll—doll—doll! You are stuffed with sawdust and you will never have a heart. *You're a doll!*"

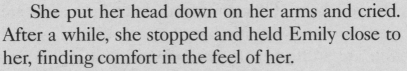
She put her head down on her arms and cried. After a while, she stopped and held Emily close to her, finding comfort in the feel of her.

"I understand why you didn't answer, Emily. I never answer when I can help it. When people are insulting me, I just look at them and *think*. Miss Minchin turns pale with rage when I do it. When I won't answer insults, everyone knows that I'm stronger than they are. And I am."

She went to her hard bed, cuddling Emily close to her.

The very next morning when she was coming from an errand, she saw the driver of a moving van stop his horses before the empty row-house next door. When she saw the beautiful, rich furniture being carried into the house, her heart beat fast. Some of the rugs and furniture looked as if they had come from India.

"And it will all be just on the other side of my wall," she said to herself. "I shall feel as if the new people are friends. I hope a head will look out of their attic window when I look out of mine."

Later, she saw the father of the Large Family walk across the square and give directions to the workmen.

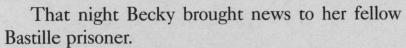
That night Becky brought news to her fellow Bastille prisoner.

"It's a gentleman from India that's comin' to live next door, miss," she said. "He's very rich, an' he's ill, an' Guy Lawrence's papa is his lawyer. He's had a lot of trouble, an' it's made him ill an' low in his mind and he hasn't got no family at all."

Sara watched the house very carefully for several weeks. Finally, a carriage stopped there one day. Guy Lawrence's father got out, then a nurse in uniform, then two men-servants. They helped a thin, sad-faced man from the carriage and carried him up the steps. Shortly after this, a doctor's carriage arrived, and the doctor went in—plainly to take care of the thin, ill man.

CHAPTER ELEVEN

Ram Dass

When she could get up to her room in time, Sara would climb on the old table and get her head out the window to watch the sunset. The drifting clouds would change to pink or crimson or snow-white or purple or pale dove-gray. Sometimes they made islands with blue or emerald-green lakes. Sometimes great mountains jutted into strange, lost seas. Sometimes it seemed that, perhaps, she could float away from her attic with them.

There was such a sunset as this a few days after the Indian gentleman was brought to his new home. She mounted her table and stood looking out. It was a wonderful moment. There were floods of gold covering the west. A deep, rich yellow light filled the air. The birds flying across the tops of the houses showed black against it.

"It's a splendid sunset," said Sara softly to herself. "It makes me feel as if something strange is just going to happen. The splendid ones always make me feel like that."

Suddenly she heard a squeaky chattering coming from the window of the next attic. Was someone else coming to see the sunset? Sara watched as the person emerged. She saw a dark face with gleaming eyes beneath a white turban. *It is a Lascar!* Sara said to herself quickly. She recognized a Lascar, a native Indian manservant, from her life in India. The sound she had heard came from a small monkey snuggled in his arms.

He looked toward her and Sara smiled. He showed gleaming white teeth as he smiled back.

The monkey suddenly broke loose, ran across the slate roof, and climbed down into Sara's room. She called to the Lascar, feeling glad that she remembered some of the language she had learned in India.

"Will he let me catch him?"

The Lascar looked delighted when she spoke his native Indian language.

"I am called Ram Dass. If Missee Sahib will permit, I will cross the roof to her room and get the unworthy little animal."

"Come," Sara said. "He seems frightened."

Ram Dass came across the roof and into her room. He caught the monkey after a short chase. Sara knew that he had noticed the shabbiness of the room, but he pretended he didn't. He thanked her, adding that the man he worked for was very ill and would have been sad if the monkey had been lost. Before he left, he bowed and thanked her again.

Left alone, Sara remembered her time in India, surrounded by servants. She knew that here she would always be a servant. Then she straightened her thin little body and lifted her head.

"Whatever comes," she said, "if I am in rags, I can be a princess inside even if no one knows it."

The next morning Sara was putting the school books in order. She was thinking that if Miss Minchin knew that she, Sara—whose toes were almost sticking out of her boots—was a princess, she would be shocked. The thought of Miss Minchin's shocked face made her laugh.

"What are you laughing at, you rude child?" Miss Minchin exclaimed. She boxed Sara's ears several times for no reason.

Sara's cheeks were red and stinging from the blows she had received. But she remembered that a princess must be polite.

"I was thinking," she answered.

"And what were you thinking?" demanded Miss Minchin.

Jessie giggled and nudged Lavinia. All the girls looked up from their books to listen.

"I was thinking," Sara answered, "how surprised you would be if you found out that I really *was* a princess."

"Beg my pardon and go back to the kitchen," cried Miss Minchin.

Sara made a little bow.

"Excuse me for laughing if it was impolite," Sara said, "but I won't beg your pardon for thinking."

She walked out of the room.

"Did you see her?" Jessie whispered. "I wouldn't be at all surprised if she *did* turn out to be a princess!"

CHAPTER TWELVE

The Other Side of the Wall

Sara had become fond of the Large Family because they looked happy. Now she became fond of the gentleman next door because he looked unhappy. She heard Cook discussing him with one of the maids.

"He's an Englishman who went to live in India. He had some kind of money troubles with mines and then he thought he was ruined forever. Diamond mines." She looked at Sara with a nasty grin. "He almost died of the shock and the jungle fever. And ever since he's been in poor health. But he's getting diamonds from the mine, now, and he's rich again."

"He was like my papa," Sara thought, "but he didn't die like my papa did. And if he has a little girl, she isn't a poor servant."

Now, when she was coming back from errands at night, she would look over at his house and wish him a good night.

"Perhaps kind thoughts reach people through walls," she whispered. "Perhaps you feel a little warm and comforted, and don't know why, when I am standing here in the cold and hoping you will get well and happy again." She would go away feeling comforted and warmer herself.

* * *

Sara knew that the father of the Large Family often went to see the gentleman next door. She also knew that some of the children visited, too. What she did not know was that the children had told the gentleman about her, although they did not know her name.

The Large Family's real name was Carmichael. The father, Mr. Carmichael, was the gentleman's lawyer. The gentleman, who also had a real name— Mr. Carrisford—enjoyed the children's visits, for

they cheered him up. They told him all about The-Little-Girl-who-was-not-a-beggar because he was fond of children. And Ram Dass told him about the poor little girl who lived in the gloomy attic. Little did they know that this was Sara, who was secretly fond of them all.

One evening Mr. Carrisford sat with Mr. Carmichael in the library.

"Do you think it is possible that this child we are searching for could be living like the poor little soul next door?" asked Mr. Carrisford.

"If the child who was at Madame Pascal's school in Paris is the one you are looking for, she was adopted by a wealthy Russian family. But I will go to their home in Russia and find out for sure if she is the one," replied Mr. Carmichael.

"The name was different…"

"Madame Pascal used the name Carew instead of Crewe, but the child's story is very much like ours. An English officer in India had placed his motherless little girl at the school. He died suddenly after losing his fortune. Are you sure Captain Crewe's child was left at a school in Paris?" Mr. Carmichael asked.

"I only knew that the child had been sent to school somewhere. But her mother was French and it seems likely that she would go there."

"Yes," Mr. Carmichael said, "it seems likely."

"I must find her," Mr. Carrisford said. "This sudden change of fortune at the mines has made us wealthy, and poor Crewe's child may be begging in the street!" He groaned. "Ralph Crewe trusted me—he loved me. And he died thinking that I had ruined him!"

"Don't blame yourself so bitterly."

"I blame myself for running away like a thief. I could not face my best friend and tell him I had ruined him and his child."

"You were in a hospital and out of your mind with jungle fever," Mr. Carmichael said.

Mr. Carrisford dropped his head in his hands.

"And when I came to myself, poor Crewe was dead. And I didn't remember anything about the child, not even her name. But I must find her."

"I will go to Russia," Mr. Carmichael said. "We will find her."

The ill gentleman looked up at his lawyer. "I dream sometimes that Crewe is asking me where his little girl is. We must find her. We must."

On the other side of the wall, Sara was sitting in her attic talking to Melchisedec, who had come out for his evening meal.

"It has been hard to be a princess today, Melchisedec," she said. "It has been harder than usual. It gets harder as the weather grows colder and the streets get sloppier. When Lavinia laughed at my muddy skirt as I passed her in the hall, I only just bit back a remark in time. You can't sneer back at people like that if you are a princess, but it's hard. It was a cold afternoon, Melchisedec. And it's a cold night."

She put her head down in her arms.

"Oh, Papa," she whispered, "what a long time it seems since I was with you."

CHAPTER THIRTEEN

One of the People

The winter was a bad one. Sara tramped through snow or mud when she went on her errands. Sometimes the fog was so thick that the street lamps burned all day. On such days the windows of the two houses Sara watched looked warm and cozy. But the attic was gloomy.

There were no longer sunsets or sunrises or stars in her window. It was dark at four o'clock. The women in the kitchen were cross. Becky was driven like a little slave.

"If it warn't for you an' the Bastille," Becky said to Sara one night, "an' bein' the prisoner in the next jail cell, I would die. The missus is more like the head jailer every day. The cook, she's like one of the under-jailers. Tell me some more, please, miss. I feel warmer when you tell stories."

Sara and Becky bundled up in her blanket and Sara told a story about a monkey from the jungle.

"What you have to do with your mind, when your body is miserable, is to make it think of something else," Sara explained.

"Can you do it, miss?" asked Becky.

"Only sometimes," Sara answered honestly. "When I can, I say to myself, 'I am a princess, and because I am a princess nothing can hurt me or make me uncomfortable.' "

But one cold, rainy day, Sara found she couldn't think of being a princess. She was sent out on errands again and again. Her shabby clothes became wet through, and her worn-out shoes were full of water. Her dinner had been taken away as a punishment. She was so cold and hungry and tired that she couldn't stop her thin body from shivering.

"Suppose I had dry clothes," she thought. "Suppose I had good shoes and a thick coat. And suppose—just suppose—that just when I was near a bakery where they sold hot buns I would find a sixpence. If I did, I would go into the shop and buy six of the hottest buns and eat them all without stopping."

Some very odd things happen in this world sometimes. And an odd thing happened to Sara.

As the muddy water seeped into her broken shoes, she looked down to avoid the heavy mud. She saw something shining in the gutter. It was a silver coin—a tiny coin walked upon by many feet, but still with enough spirit left to shine a little. It was not quite a sixpence, but the next thing to it—a fourpenny piece.

"Oh!" she gasped. "It is true! It is true!"

She was outside a baker's shop, and a plump, motherly woman was just then taking out a tray of hot buns. The scent of warm bread made Sara feel almost faint.

She started up the shop steps. Then she stopped. A little figure more forlorn even than herself huddled there. It was not much more than a bundle of rags, with bare, muddy feet, and a dirty face peeping out from under tangled hair.

Sara clutched her fourpenny piece and hesitated. Then she asked, "Are you hungry?"

The child shuffled her rags. "Ain't I jist?"

"When did you eat?" asked Sara.

"Never got nothin' to eat today."

Though she was hungry and sick at heart, Sara was thinking to herself, "When princesses were poor and driven from their thrones, they still shared with the common people—if they met one poorer and hungrier than themselves. This is one of the people and she is hungrier than I am. Buns are a penny each. It won't be enough but it will be better than nothing."

She went into the warm shop. "Four penny buns, if you please."

The woman put six in a paper bag.

"I said four, if you please," Sara explained. "I have only fourpence."

"I'll throw in two extra," said the kind-faced woman. "You look hungry enough to eat them."

Sara thanked her and went out. The beggar girl was still huddled on the step, rubbing away tears with her dirty hand.

Sara took out one of the buns. "See," she said, putting the bun in the ragged lap, "this is nice and hot."

The child snatched up the bun and began to cram it into her mouth. It was too full to let her say thanks.

Sara took out three more buns for the girl.

"She is hungrier than I am," Sara reminded herself. "She's starving."

But Sara's hand trembled when she put down the fourth bun.

"I'm not starving," Sara said—and she put down the fifth.

The little street beggar was still gulping down the bread when Sara turned and walked home.

At that moment the baker-woman looked out of her shop window.

"Well!" she exclaimed. "If that young'un hasn't given her buns to a beggar child! It wasn't because she wasn't hungry herself, either."

She went to the door.

"Are you still hungry?" she asked the beggar child.

"I'm allus hungry," was the answer, "but it ain't as bad as it was."

"Come in here," said the woman.

The child got up and shuffled in.

"Get yourself warm," said the woman, pointing to a fire in the back room. "And when you're hungry, you can come in here. I'm blest if I won't give you bread for that young'un's sake."

Sara found some comfort in her remaining bun. As she walked along she broke off small pieces and ate them slowly to make them last longer.

It was dark when she reached the square and the lighted windows comforted her. At the Carmichael home, the children were telling their father good-bye. She heard someone say, "Will Russia be covered with snow and ice everywhere?"

"If you find the little girl, give her our love," shouted Guy Clarence, jumping up and down as the father hurried out to his carriage.

"I wonder who the little girl is that he's going to look for," Sara thought.

She went into Miss Minchin's, lugging her heavy basket and feeling faint and shaky from cold and hunger. At the very same time, Mr. Carmichael was on his way to the station to take the train to Russia to search for the lost little daughter of Captain Crewe.

CHAPTER FOURTEEN

What Melchisedec Heard and Saw

While Sara was out on her errands, Melchisedec was sniffing about the attic. He was frightened by a sound on the roof and ran to hide in his hole.

The skylight was opened and two men entered the room. One was Ram Dass and the other was a young man who was Mr. Carrisford's secretary.

The secretary caught a glimpse of Melchisedec's vanishing tail. "Was that a rat?" he whispered.

"Yes, a rat, Sahib," Ram Dass whispered back. "There are many in the walls."

"Ugh!" exclaimed the young man. "It is a wonder the child is not terrified of them."

"The child is the friend of all things, Sahib," Ram Dass answered. "She is not as other children. The sparrows come at her call. The rat she has fed and tamed in her loneliness. The poor scullery maid comes to her for comfort. By the evil mistress of the house she is treated like a slave. But she has the manner of a princess!"

"You are sure that she will not return? She would be frightened, and Mr. Carrisford's plan would be spoiled," said the secretary.

"She has gone out with her basket and may be gone for hours," answered Ram Dass.

The secretary began to walk slowly and softly around the little room, quickly writing down notes on his tablet.

"It is a strange way of doing this thing," he said. "Who planned it?"

"The first thought was mine," Ram Dass said with a bow. "That is so. And it seemed then but a dream. But the Sahib became interested in the child. At last he began to please himself with the thought of making her life better. And so these are his wishes and his plans."

"You think that it can be done while she sleeps?" asked the young man.

"I can move as if my feet were of velvet," Ram Dass replied. "And she sleeps soundly from being so tired. If someone passes to me the things through the window, I can do all. When she awakens she will think a magician has been here."

"I think I have made notes enough, so we can go now," the secretary said. "The Sahib Carrisford has a warm heart. It is a thousand pities that he has not found the lost child."

"If he should find her, his strength would be restored to him," said Ram Dass. "His God may lead her to him yet."

They slipped back through the window.

Melchisedec came out and looked around. He hoped that even such alarming human beings as these might have carried crumbs in their pockets and left one or two of them behind.

CHAPTER FIFTEEN

The Magic

When Sara went into the kitchen, the cook was angry. "Why didn't you just stay out *all* night?" she snapped.

"May I have something to eat?" Sara asked faintly. "I had no dinner."

"And you'll get nothing this late. Did you expect me to save it for you?"

Sara had to stop and rest several times while climbing the stairs to her attic. When she reached it, Ermengarde was there.

"Oh, Sara," she exclaimed, "you do look tired."

Sara stood with her head turned toward the stairs. "Shhh. I think it's Miss Minchin."

Ermengarde put out the candle.

"She's scolding Becky," Sara whispered.

"You thief!" they heard her say. "Stealing half a meat pie!"

"It warn't me, mum," said Becky, sobbing. "I never laid a finger on it."

"Don't tell lies," Miss Minchin screamed.

They heard her box Becky's ears. Becky ran into her attic, crying, and Miss Minchin went back downstairs.

"The wicked, cruel thing!" Sara cried. "Cook takes things herself and then says Becky steals them. She doesn't! And Becky's so hungry that she eats crusts out of the trash can!" She hid her face in her hands and burst into tears.

Ermengarde lit the candle and looked at Sara.

"Sara—I don't want to be rude, but—are you ever hungry?"

Sara forgot any pride.

"Yes," she said. "Yes. I'm hungry now."

Ermengarde gasped. "Oh, Sara! And I never knew! My aunt sent me a box full of food. I'll go and get it."

"Ermie! You will?" Sara raised her head. "May we invite the prisoner in the next cell?"

"Oh, yes," Ermengarde said. And she hurried out so quickly that she dropped her shawl.

Sara knocked on the wall and Becky appeared. Her eyes were red.

"Miss Ermengarde has a whole box of good things to eat," Sara cried. "And she's bringing it up here. Somehow, something always happens just before things get to the very worst. It is as if the Magic did it. The worst thing never quite comes. Look, Miss Ermengarde left her shawl. Let's use it for a nice red tablecloth when we set the table."

"Set the table, miss?" said Becky.

"We'll pretend!" said Sara, laughing, as she spread the shawl over the old table. "We must pretend there's a red rug on the floor. My… how soft and thick it is!"

"Oh, yes, miss," said Becky, in awe of Sara.

"What next, now?" asked Sara. She stood still with her hands over her eyes. "Something will come if I think and wait a little… The Magic will tell me."

One of Sara's favorite fancies was that on "the outside," as she called it, thoughts were waiting for someone to call them.

"There!" Sara cried, uncovering her eyes. "It has come! I must look in my old trunk I had when I was a princess."

In the old trunk the girls indeed found Magic. There were small white handkerchiefs for plates. A worn-out flower wreath from a hat and a soap dish became the centerpiece. Tissue paper was shaped into candy dishes.

"It's no longer the Bastille," said Sara. "It's a grand banquet hall where feasts are given."

"Is it, miss?" said Becky with wide eyes.

"You must pretend it," said Sara. "If you pretend it enough, you will see it."

Ermengarde giggled when she came in and saw the table. She set a large basket down and they took meat pies and fruit and chocolates out of it. Then they gathered around the table, hardly able to believe their eyes.

But they had barely taken the food in their hands when they heard a sound on the stairs. They turned pale faces toward the door, trembling.

Miss Minchin struck the door open, red with rage. She looked from the frightened faces to the feast on the table.

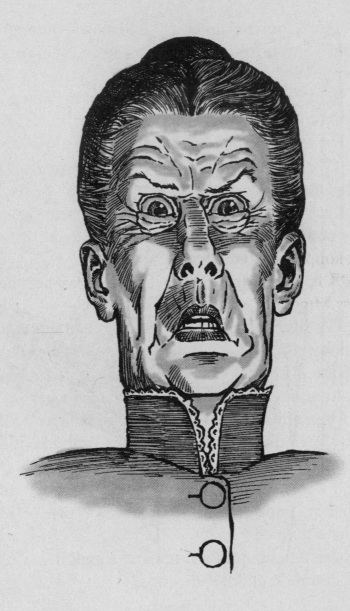

"So," she exclaimed, "Lavinia was telling the truth." She boxed Becky's ears again. "Go to your room, now!"

Becky ran. Her face was hidden in her apron and her shoulders were shaking.

Ermengarde burst into tears.

"My aunt sent me the basket of treats," she sobbed. "We were—only—going to eat."

Miss Minchin turned fiercely on Sara. "This is *your* doing. You shall have neither breakfast, dinner, nor supper tomorrow!"

"I have not had either dinner or supper today, Miss Minchin," said Sara faintly.

"Then all the better to make you remember. Ermengarde, go back to bed. You will stay there all day tomorrow. I shall write to your papa. What would he say if he knew where you are tonight?"

Miss Minchin saw something in Sara's face that made her turn. "Why do you look at me like that?" the old lady demanded.

"I was wondering," Sara answered in a low voice, "what *my* papa would say if he knew where I am tonight."

Miss Minchin flew at her and shook her.

"You rude child!" she cried.

She swept the food all in a heap back into the basket and pushed Ermengarde through the door.

Sara was left alone. The food she had seen and didn't get to eat had left her hungrier than ever.

She picked up Emily and sat with her head in her arms for some time. She felt so tired and weak that she went slowly to the bed.

"Suppose there was a bright fire in the grate, with lots of dancing flames," she murmured. "Suppose there was a soft chair and a small table near with a hot supper on it. And suppose…" She drew the thin covering over her. "Suppose this was a beautiful soft bed with warm blankets and feather pillows. Suppose… suppose…" Her eyes closed and she fell asleep.

⊹⦂❀⦂⊹

She didn't know how long she slept but she woke suddenly, aware of a sound on the roof. At first she didn't open her eyes. She felt too sleepy and too warm and comfortable. She didn't believe she was really awake.

"What a nice dream!" she murmured. "I—don't—want—to—wake—up."

She was dreaming she had blankets heaped upon her. She tried to keep her eyes closed to make it last. But a sense of light and the sound of a crackling little fire made her eyes open in spite of herself. And then she smiled.

"Oh, I haven't awakened," she whispered, looking all about her. "I'm still dreaming."

In the grate there was a blazing fire and a little brass kettle hung above it, hissing and boiling. A chair and a cloth-covered table with dishes of hot food sat near the fire. A thick crimson rug was on the floor, and on the bed were warm coverings, a silk robe, a pair of quilted slippers, and some books. The room seemed changed into fairyland.

She sat up and put her feet on the warm rug.

"It stays—real! It's bewitched—or I'm bewitched. I only think I see it all."

She knelt by the fire and held out her hands close to it—and felt the heat.

"If this were only a fire in a dream, it couldn't be hot," she cried.

She sprang up and went about touching everything. She took up the robe and put it around her shoulders.

"It's warm. It's soft!" she almost sobbed. "It's real. It must be!"

There was a note in one of the books. "To the little girl in the attic. From a friend."

She buried her face in the book and felt tears come into her eyes. "Somebody cares for me. I have a friend."

Then she hurried into Becky's room. "Oh, Becky, come!" she whispered.

Becky stood up, too surprised to speak.

Sara drew her into the warm, glowing room and shut the door.

"It's true!" Sara cried. "I've touched them all. They are real. The Magic has come and done it, Becky, while we were asleep—the Magic that won't let those worst things ever quite happen."

CHAPTER SIXTEEN

The Visitor

They sat by the warm fire and ate soup and sandwiches and muffins.

"Do you think," Becky whispered once, "it's a dream, miss?"

"No," said Sara. "You never really eat things in dreams. You only think you're going to eat them."

When they became sleepy again, Sara gave Becky one of her new blankets. As she went out of the room, Becky turned and looked about her.

"If it ain't here in the mornin', miss," she said, "it's been here tonight, anyways, an' I'll never forget it. The fire was there," pointing with her finger, "an' the table was before it. An' there was covers on your

bed, an' a warm rug on the floor, an' everythin' looked beautiful. An' "—she laid her hand on her stomach—"there was soup an' sandwiches an' muffins—there was!"

In the morning, everyone knew that the girls were being punished, but Sara and Becky were too excited to worry. Sara went down into the scullery and Becky grinned at her.

"It was there when I wakened, miss—the blanket yer give me," she whispered happily.

"So was mine," said Sara.

Sara went up to the schoolroom with a smile playing around her mouth.

"Perhaps she is pretending she has had a good breakfast," Lavinia said spitefully.

Sara's expression made Miss Minchin angry. She reminded Sara in a mean voice that she was to be punished and have nothing to eat for the whole day.

"Yes, Miss Minchin," Sara answered, still feeling full from the night before.

"Whatever happens," Sara kept saying to herself all that day, "there is a kind person somewhere who is my friend. Even if I never know who it is, I shall never again feel quite so lonely."

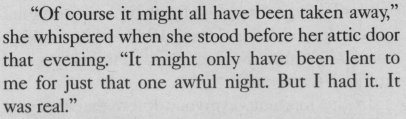

"Of course it might all have been taken away," she whispered when she stood before her attic door that evening. "It might only have been lent to me for just that one awful night. But I had it. It was real."

She opened the door and gasped in delight.

The Magic had been there again and it had done even more than before. A fire burned in the grate. Another supper was on the table with cups and plates for Becky also. There was a new, soft mattress cover and pillow on her bed. All the bare, ugly things were covered with bright materials and several large cushions were scattered about. Sara simply sat down and looked.

"I'm not the same cold, ragged, hungry Sara," she said aloud. "I'm in a fairy story come true."

Becky came as soon as Sara knocked to her.

"My, who does it, miss?" she gasped.

"I almost would rather not know, even though I want to thank them. It makes it more beautiful."

The fairy story continued. Almost every day something new was added. The attic became a beautiful little room with pictures and furniture and books. When Sara came in each evening, a nice meal was waiting.

What did her ugly daytime life matter while she was living in this wonderful fairy story at night? Sometimes, when she was scolded by Miss Minchin, she could scarcely keep from smiling.

"If you only knew!" she would say to herself.

One day a man left several packages in the hall. Sara was sent to take them into the parlor. She was looking at the address with great interest when Miss Minchin saw her.

"Take the things to the young lady to whom they belong," she said harshly.

"They belong to me," answered Sara.

"To you?" exclaimed Miss Minchin. "What do you mean?"

"They are addressed to me." She showed the address to Miss Minchin.

"It says right here. To the Little Girl in the Right-Hand Attic," said Sara.

"Open them," Miss Minchin ordered. She was looking rather uneasy.

Sara did as she was told. The packages contained pretty and comfortable clothing. There was a warm coat and hat and an umbrella. A note was pinned on the coat: "To be worn every day. Will be replaced by others when needed."

Miss Minchin was frightened. Could it be that the poor child had a relative who had found her, and might come to see about her? It would be bad if such a person had learned about the thin, shabby clothes, the scant food, and the hard work.

"Well," she said, in the voice that she hadn't used since Sara lost her father, "you may go and put the things on. After you are dressed you may come downstairs and learn your lessons in the schoolroom. You need not go out on any more errands today."

When Sara wore her new clothes into the schoolroom, the girls stopped work to look at her.

"Perhaps the diamond mines have suddenly appeared again," said Lavinia meanly.

That night Sara sat by the fire and wrote a thank-you note to the kind person who had helped her. She left it on the table. The next evening the note had been taken away, so she knew her secret Magic friend had received it.

She was reading one of her new books to Becky when they heard a sound on the roof. She climbed on a chair and raised the window. A tiny shivering figure crouched on the snow outside.

"It's the monkey that belongs to the Lascar," she cried out. "Oh, it's too cold for him to be out."

She reached out and he let her lift him through the window.

"Nice monkey! Nice monkey!" she crooned, kissing his funny head.

"What will you do with him, miss?" Becky asked.

"I shall let him sleep with me tonight, and then I'll take him back to the Lascar and the Indian gentleman tomorrow."

And when she went to bed she made him a nest at her feet, and he slept there as if he were a baby.

CHAPTER SEVENTEEN

"It Is the Child!"

The next afternoon, three of the Carmichael children sat with Mr. Carrisford in his library.

"It won't be long before Papa comes home," one of the girls said. "May we talk about the little girl you are searching for? We call her the Little Un-fairy Princess because, though she is not exactly like a fairy, she will be so rich when she is found that she will be like a princess in a fairy tale."

"There's a cab!" the little boy shouted. "It's stopping before the door. It's Papa!"

The children ran to the windows to look out.

"But there's no little girl," said the boy sadly.

The children then tumbled into the hall. From his chair in the library, Mr. Carrisford could hear them jumping up and down, and being caught up and kissed. Then his lawyer, Mr. Carmichael, came into the room alone.

"What news?" Mr. Carrisford looked up anxiously. "Did you find the child in Russia?"

"I did. She's not Captain Crewe's child. Her name is Emily Carew."

"The search has to begin all over again," said Mr. Carrisford in a weary voice.

"Yes," Mr. Carmichael replied. "We have searched the schools in Paris. Let's look at the schools here in London."

At that moment, Ram Dass came into the room. "Sahib," he said, "the child you felt pity for has come. She brings back the monkey who had again run away to her attic. I have asked that she remain. It was my thought that it would please you to see and speak with her."

Mr. Carrisford smiled and waved his hand to Ram Dass. "Yes, I should like to see her. Bring her in." Then he turned to Mr. Carmichael. "Ram Dass told me of this child's misery, and we made a plan to carry good things to her attic room."

Then Sara came into the room, carrying the monkey in her arms. She curtsied. "It was too late to bring this monkey back last night. I knew you were ill and might not like to be disturbed."

"That was very thoughtful of you," the gentleman said.

Sara looked toward Ram Dass, who stood near the door.

"Shall I give him to the Lascar?" she asked.

"How do you know he is a Lascar?" asked the gentleman, smiling.

"Oh, I know Lascars," Sara said, handing over the monkey. "I was born in India."

Mr. Carrisford sat upright suddenly.

"You were born in India," he exclaimed, "were you? Come here." He held out his hand.

Sara went to him and laid her hand in his.

"You live next door?" he asked.

"Yes. I live at Miss Minchin's seminary."

"But you are not one of her pupils?"

Sara hesitated a moment.

"At first I was a pupil, but now—"

"You *were* a pupil!" Mr. Carrisford sank back. "What do you mean by 'at first,' my child?"

"When I was first taken there by my papa."

"Where is your papa now?" he asked.

"He died," said Sara, "and he lost all his money, so there was no one to take care of me or to pay Miss Minchin."

"Carmichael!" the gentleman cried out loudly. "Ask her."

"How did your father lose his money?" Mr. Carmichael quietly asked Sara.

"He did not lose it himself," Sara answered slowly. She wondered why they were asking her such things. "A friend lost it."

"And what was your father's name?" the Indian gentleman asked, breathing rapidly.

"His name was Ralph Crewe. Captain Crewe."

"Carmichael," the gentleman gasped, "it is the child—the child!"

Sara looked at Mr. Carmichael. "What child am I?" she whispered.

"This gentleman was your father's friend," Mr. Carmichael explained. "But, you see, he did not really lose your papa's money. He only thought the diamond mines were a failure. He almost died of jungle fever, too, and long before he became well your poor papa was dead. We have been looking for you for two years."

Sara put her hand up to her forehead, and her mouth trembled. She spoke as if she were in a dream.

"And I was at Miss Minchin's all the while," she whispered. "Just on the other side of the wall."

Just then, all the Carmichael children came into the room with their happy, rosy mother. They had heard the glad news from outside the door.

"It's The-Little-Girl-who-is-not-a-beggar!" the boy whispered.

Mrs. Carmichael took Sara in her arms.

"My dear, Mr. Carrisford believed Captain Crewe's daughter was at school in France. When he saw you pass by on your errands, he did not dream that you were his friend's poor child. But he was sorry for you and he told Ram Dass to climb into your attic window and make you comfortable with food and pretty things."

"You made the fairy story!" Sara cried out, hardly able to believe what had just happened. "And to think that I only meant to bring the monkey back."

CHAPTER EIGHTEEN

"I Tried Not to Be"

Sara went and knelt by Mr. Carrisford.

"It is you who were my friend." She kissed his thin hand.

Mr. Carrisford was stronger already. He had the lost girl and she was not to return to the seminary. She would stay at his house. He would send Mr. Carmichael to arrange matters with Miss Minchin.

"I'm glad I need not go back," said Sara, "for Miss Minchin will be very angry that I am here."

But Miss Minchin *had* found that Sara went to Mr. Carrisford's house and she hurried over to bring her back.

Sara was sitting on a footstool close to the gentleman's knee when Miss Minchin was brought into the library. The old lady looked angrily at Sara as she introduced herself.

"So *you* are Miss Minchin?" Mr. Carrisford said sternly.

"I am, sir."

"My lawyer, Mr. Carmichael, was just going to see you," he said.

"Your lawyer?" Miss Minchin said. "I do not understand. I have just learned that one of my pupils—a charity pupil—has come into your home. I shall take her back immediately."

She turned on Sara. "Go home at once," she ordered. "You shall be severely punished."

Mr. Carrisford drew Sara to his side and held her trembling hand in his.

"She is not going."

"Not going?" Miss Minchin repeated.

"No," said Mr. Carrisford. "Her home will be with me."

"With you, sir! What does this mean?"

Mr. Carmichael stepped forward and explained to Miss Minchin about Captain Crewe's fortune and Mr. Carrisford's own search for Sara.

"The diamond mines!" Miss Minchin gasped out. "Sara's fortune."

"There are not many princesses, Miss Minchin, who are richer than your little charity pupil will be. Mr. Carrisford has found her at last, and he will keep her," said the lawyer.

Miss Minchin was silly enough to try to get back what she had lost through her cruelty.

"He found her under my care. If it weren't for me, she would have starved in the streets."

"She was starving in your attic," Mr. Carrisford said angrily.

"Captain Crewe left her in my charge," she argued. "The law will make her stay with me."

"The law will do nothing of the sort," Mr. Carmichael said. "Mr. Carrisford will see that Sara may do as she wishes."

Miss Minchin sounded almost as if she were begging. "Sara, I ask you to come back. I have not spoiled you, but I have always been fond of you."

Sara was thinking of the day when she had been told that she belonged to nobody, and was in danger of being turned out into the street. She was thinking of the cold, hungry hours she had spent alone in the attic.

Sara gave Miss Minchin the quiet, clear look the cruel woman hated. "*Have* you been fond of me, Miss Minchin?" she said. "I did not know that."

A hot flush spread over Miss Minchin's hard, angry face.

"You will never see your friends again," she began. "I will see that Ermengarde and Lottie are kept away—"

"Excuse me," Mr. Carmichael said, "but she will see anyone she wishes to see. The parents of Miss Crewe's fellow pupils will be happy to have them visit her here."

At last Miss Minchin saw that she had lost and turned to leave. "I suppose," she said to Sara, "that you feel now that you are a princess again."

"I—*tried* not to be anything else," Sara answered in a low voice—"even when I was coldest and hungriest—I tried not to be."

·⁓⧓⧓⁓·

That evening, when the pupils were sitting before the fire in the schoolroom, Ermengarde came in with a letter in her hand and a strange sort of excited smile on her face.

"What *is* the matter?" cried two or three voices.

"I got a letter—from *Sara*," said Ermengarde.

"Where is she?" Jessie shrieked.

"Next door," said Ermengarde, "with the gentleman from India. The mines are full of diamonds, and half of them belong to Sara. And they belonged to her when she was living in the attic, and was hungry, and had the cook ordering her about. And her father's friend didn't know where to find her but he found her this afternoon and she will be more a princess than she ever was. And I'm going to see her tomorrow afternoon. And so is Lottie. So there!"

Becky, who had heard Sara's story in the kitchen, went to look at the little magic room before it was taken away—before the attic would be bare and empty again. She was glad for Sara's sake, but still she went up the last flight of stairs with tears in her eyes. There would be no fire tonight, and no supper. And the saddest thing was that her friend would be gone.

She choked down a sob as she pushed the attic door open. Then she gave a low cry.

The fire was blazing, the supper was waiting, and Ram Dass was there smiling at her.

"Missee Sahib did not wish that you should go to sleep unhappy. The Sahib asks you to come to him tomorrow. You are to live in his home now, and be the special helper and companion of Missee Sahib."

He made a little bow and slipped through the skylight, leaving the delighted little lady.

CHAPTER NINETEEN

Anne

In a month's time Mr. Carrisford was well. He found pleasure in the things he could do for Sara. Every day she found beautiful new flowers growing in her room and many little gifts tucked under her pillows. He and Sara became fond of each other and often sat alone to read or talk. This was the best time for both of them.

One evening Sara sat gazing into the fire.

"What are you 'supposing,' Sara?" he asked.

Sara looked up. "I was remembering a hungry day, and a child I saw."

"But you had a great many hungry days," he said sadly. "Which hungry day was it?"

Sara told him the story of the fourpence she picked from the mud, and the child who was hungrier than herself. She told it quite simply, but it brought tears to his eyes.

"I was thinking I should like to do something," she added.

"What is it?" he asked.

"I was wondering if I could go see the baker-woman. I want to ask if she will give food to any hungry children she sees, and then send the bills to me. May I do that?"

"You shall do it tomorrow morning," he said.

"Thank you," said Sara. "You see, I know what it is to be hungry, and it is very hard when one cannot even pretend it away."

"Yes, yes, my dear," said the gentleman. "Just remember that you are a princess now."

"Yes," said Sara, smiling, "and I can scatter gold to the people. I can give them bread."

The next morning, Miss Minchin saw Sara and Mr. Carrisford, warm in soft furs, get into their carriage. And there was Becky, pink and smiling, carrying extra wraps to the carriage for Sara.

When Sara entered the baker's shop, the baker-woman looked at her.

"I'm sure that I remember you, miss," the baker-woman said. "And yet—"

"Yes," said Sara, "once you gave me six buns for fourpence, and—"

"And you gave five of 'em to a beggar child," the woman broke in on her. "You look rosier and—well, better than you did that—that—"

"I am better, thank you," said Sara. "And I am much happier—and I have come to ask you to do something for me."

"Why, bless you, yes! What can I do?"

Sara told her what she wanted.

"Why, bless me, it'll be a pleasure to me to do it. I am a working woman myself an' can't afford to do much. But I've given away many a bit of bread since that wet afternoon, just from thinking of you—an' how wet an' cold you was, an' how hungry you looked. An' yet you gave away those hot buns as if you was a princess."

"She was even hungrier than I was," Sara said.

"She was starving," said the woman. "Many's the time she's told me of it since—how she sat there in the wet an' cold, and felt as if a wolf was a-tearing at her poor young insides."

"Oh, have you seen her since then?" exclaimed Sara. "Do you know where she is?"

"Yes, I do," answered the woman, smiling more than ever. "Why, she's in that there back room, miss. An' a decent girl she's turned out, an' such a help to me in the shop an' in the kitchen."

She called and a girl came out from the back of the shop. It was the beggar-child, now clean and neatly dressed, and looking as if she had not been hungry for a long time.

"You see," said the woman, "I told her to come when she was hungry, and when she'd come I'd give her odd jobs to do. An' I found she was willing, and somehow I got to like her. So I've given her a place an' a home. Her name's Anne. She has no other."

The children stood and looked at each other for a few minutes. Then Sara took her hand out of her muff and held it out, and Anne took it. They looked straight into each other's eyes.

"I am so glad," Sara said. "Perhaps you may be the one to give the bread to the children. Perhaps you would like to do it because you know what it is to be hungry, too."

"Yes, miss," said the girl.

And somehow Sara felt as if Anne understood her, though she said so little, and only stood still and looked and looked after her as she went out of the shop with the gentleman, and they got into the carriage and drove away.

THE END

FRANCES HODGSON BURNETT

Frances Hodgson was born in Manchester, England, in 1849. Like the characters in her stories, Sara Crewe from *A Little Princess* and Mary Lennox from *The Secret Garden*, Frances lost her father when she was very young. His death was hard on the family, and they became quite poor. They left England when Frances was 16 years old, moving to an uncle's small farm near Knoxville, Tennessee.

Frances knew early in her life that she wanted to be a writer. She began publishing stories in magazines while still in her teens. These sales helped support her family. In 1873, she married Dr. Swan Burnett and lived in Washington, DC, and then in England. They had two sons, Lionel and Vivian.

Frances Hodgson Burnett wrote many plays and more than 40 novels for adults. Her most famous and beloved books, however, were three that she wrote for children—*Little Lord Fauntleroy* (1886), *A Little Princess* (1905), and *The Secret Garden* (1911).

Burnett became an American citizen, but still traveled and lived at times in England. She spent her later years in New York, and died in 1924.